LOCKERBIE WRITERS' ANTHOLOGY

Stories and Poems from

Annandale and Eskdale

Edited by Kerrie

and Godfrey Newham

Illustrated by Lewanna Stewart

Foreword by Bryan Armstrong, Editor – DnG

Media Publishing Group

Steph Newham .

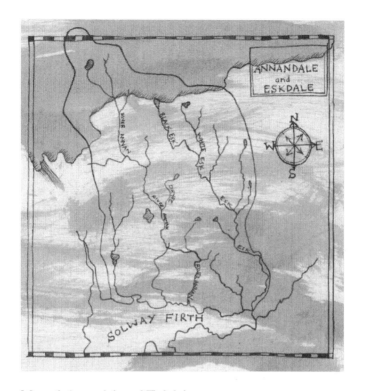

Map of Annandale and Eskdale

TABLE OF CONTENTS

TABLE OF ILLUSTRATIONS

ACKNOWLEDGEMENTS

Thank you to everyone who has supported the publication of this book. The list is endless, but we must give a mention to some of the kind individuals who have gifted their time, efforts or resources to us: Lewanna Stewart for her beautiful illustrations; Bryan Armstrong for the foreword; the students and staff on the University of Glasgow's MLitt Creative Writing who have assisted and advised Kerrie as she has put this project together; and the staff at the King's Arms Hotel, Lockerbie, for providing a space for our meetings and for serving teas and coffees with a smile.

Special thanks also go to Marian Dawber and all of the staff at Lockerbie Library for offering us a venue for the launch of this book, assisting us with all aspects of planning and marketing for this event, running the creative writing workshops in spring 2015 which were responsible for bringing several new members to Lockerbie Writers, and for all of their ongoing support.

This book could not have been created without the immeasurable efforts of all members of Lockerbie Writers, both in producing breathtaking pieces of writing, and in helping with every facet of the editing and publication process. Their enthusiasm and talent shines through on every page of this book. Thanks also go to the families and friends of every member for proofreading, providing a sympathetic ear, and for bringing us hot drinks and biscuits during the longest evenings of editing.

A final thank you goes to you for picking up this book. We hope that you enjoy it.

INTRODUCTION

Kerrie McKinnel

Writing is a difficult and often solitary process: staring at the blank page, pen hovering, waiting for inspiration – or, more likely, fingers poised above the computer keyboard with email notifications pinging in the background. Without deadlines or moral support for motivation, it can feel like an impossible journey.

In May 2015, having recently completed my first year studying towards an MLitt Creative Writing and feeling lost without classes and deadlines, I went on the search for motivation. After attending a series of writing workshops in Lockerbie Library, I learned of the existence of Lockerbie Writers.

A writing group has run in Lockerbie for many years. It is a diverse group with a wide variety of backgrounds, interests, and writing styles – as you'll see when you read this book. The range of stories which spring from the group following simple prompts never ceases to amaze me.

In winter 2015, I began to consider my upcoming university project. Coincidently, Lockerbie Writers had been discussing the production of an anthology of their work. Armed with my own personal motivation in the form of an assessment deadline, I offered to compile the anthology as my project.

As a start point, I gave the group one prompt: to produce writing which related to our home region of Annandale and Eskdale. The results were astounding: from ghost stories to fairy tales, historical fiction to funny anecdotes. I soon found myself compiling a book of almost every genre.

Writing is a difficult and often solitary process, but it doesn't have to be that way. One year ago, I didn't even know that Lockerbie Writers existed; now, I have them to thank for the prompts which have encouraged me to write a number of short stories (some of which are featured in this book), and for all of the lessons I've learned whilst compiling this book. Since joining I've also completed the initial draft of my very first novel, an achievement which I may not have reached without their support and suggestions.

I hope you enjoy reading this book as much as we've enjoyed writing it. Dip in and out; take your time. Let our experiences and contemplations fill your mind with ideas and colours. Be whisked away to worlds of fairy tale dragons, roaring rivers, and ballroom dancing!

If you enjoy reading this, please get in touch to let us know or to leave a review. Pass this book on; share it; spread the stories.

If you're a reader, keep on reading. If you're a writer, why not have a look for your nearest writers' group? It might just be the best thing you'll ever do.

FOREWORD

Bryan Armstrong, Editor, Annandale Herald/DnG Media

It is often remarked that you never fully appreciate the people and attractions close to your own home.

That is certainly not the case with members of Lockerbie Writers, the group which has completed this excellent first anthology featuring short stories and poetry, which provides a delightful insight into Annandale and Eskdale, past and present. In an era when the compressed language of social media is in vogue, it is refreshing to read these carefully crafted pages, reflecting on the beauty, heritage and character of our district, once described in a visitor guidebook as 'Scotland in miniature.'

The enthusiasm of the contributors, who meet in the Kings Arms, Lockerbie, can clearly be seen through their work.

By gathering regularly, they provide a supportive critique of other members' work and, in the process, motivate each other and improve understanding of creative writing.

Playing no small part in the development of the group - and this volume - is Kerrie McKinnel, a student on the University of Glasgow's MLitt Creative Writing course, who early on saw the benefits of writers working and learning together. At twenty-eight she is one of the youngest members of the close-knit group, whose members are drawn from varied walks of life, age groups and backgrounds.

The anthology was something which the group had been considering for some time but it only started to take shape at the end of 2015 when Kerrie took up the challenge of pulling the publication together as part of a university project. A mixture of genres and writing styles in the anthology reflects the diversity of Lockerbie Writers.

Among the topics covered are the River Annan, Lochmaben's Castle Loch, gardening, farming and the experience of living in a small town like Lockerbie.

There are stories from present day and the past, accounts of ghosts, fairy tales and more historical pieces.

The group have also been lucky enough to receive the support of up-and-coming local illustrator Lewanna Stewart, who provided the cover illustration and others featured inside.

I understand there has been much interest and expectation in Lockerbie as the anthology has taken shape, including support from the team at the town's library.

At the Annandale Herald, and its sister DnG Media newspapers, we share the group's passion for the printed word and aim to cover some of their activities in forthcoming issues.

I'm delighted to commend this anthology to readers.

LIFE, LOVE AND LOSS IN SOUTH-WEST SCOTLAND

First a Puncture

Kerrie McKinnel

First a puncture, then the lawnmower died. At least nothing else could go wrong - or could it?

Muddy water soaked through the knees of Martha's jeans, chilling her and making that last chocolate hobnob seem even more inviting, but she had to get this done. No way was she phoning Percy again. It'd been embarrassing enough when he'd shown up to sort the puncture, all teeth as he'd grinned and ruffled Georgia's hair.

'Daddy, car's broke.'

'Don't worry, pet. Your old dad's here to save the day.'

It was upsetting to see the way Georgia lit up around her dad. Of course Martha wanted them to have a good relationship, but it would've been nice to get a little recognition too. She was the one who spent her life cooking, cleaning, and doing ninety-five percent of the childcare. Percy spent the week messing around with computers at his office job in

Dumfries, and then took Georgia for a few hours on a Saturday and suddenly he was a superhero.

Well, this time Martha needed absolutely zero help from any man, in particular her ex-husband. She would fix this stupid lawnmower if it was the end of her. Jamming the screwdriver in between the blades, she wrestled it backwards and forwards. There must be something stuck in it, she thought. She'd been flying across the grass just fine, and then, *thunk*.

'Mummy?'

Martha looked up to see her little girl scurrying across the half-cut lawn, a small plastic doll in her hands.

'Mummy, she's broke.'

'Here, let me see.' Martha inspected the doll, who was decidedly headless. She tapped the top of the neck. 'Georgie, where's this bit?'

The little girl let out a wail. 'Mummy, fix her.'

'I'm not sure I can right now. Here, run back inside and see if you can find her head.'

'But Daddy would fix her.' The tears were starting.

Martha's lip quivered. 'Even Daddy couldn't fix Dolly if he didn't have her head.'

'That's not true. I want Daddy. Make Daddy fix her.'

'Please, Georgia. Mummy's busy right now. I'll be in in a minute.'

As she watched her daughter trail back into the house, Martha let out a sigh and wiped her forehead with the back of her oily hand. First the puncture, then the lawnmower, and now this. She tried to remember where the doll had been last, and then it came to her: Percy's house. Georgia was there yesterday. She must have broken Dolly's head off while he wasn't watching, and then he'd sent the stupid thing back like that. He'd have been the one to pack up her toys at the end of the afternoon. There was no way that he wouldn't have seen it.

Her screwdriver attacked the lawnmower with renewed force. She jabbed and scraped at the thing, not even interested now in whether she was fixing it or doing more damage. How could he be so useless? Georgia loved that doll. As soon as she got inside, she would phone him and ...

Pop.

A perfectly-formed doll's head flew out from between the blades and landed on the mud at her feet. Martha picked it up and turned it around to make sure that it was the one. It must have come off when Georgia was playing in the garden earlier.

'Mummy?' came the cry from inside.

'Coming, Georgie.'

Martha gave the lawnmower a try – it revved up straight away. Smiling, she tucked the doll's head into her pocket. She would find somewhere suitable to drop it when she next took Georgia to her dad's house, then they would see who was their daughter's favourite.

First a Puncture

Hogmanay Blues

Paula Nicolson

In memory of Margaret and Edward Gilfillan.

As I sipped a dram of kindness,
the Lockerbie bells sounded out
and bid farewell to Old Year's Night, for old times'
sake.

Watching Hogmanay Live
with stale shortbread and pop,
was not the teenage life I'd dreamt of on a stormy
Hogmanay night.

Ma Granny, pished on whisky
coughed her teeth into a glass,
and her intoxicated breath sent her budgie to its
grave.

A neighbour knocked and shouted
'Lang may your lum reek!'

and staggered in with coal, beer and bun tucked under
his flabby arm.

'Don't let her be the first footing,' he slurred,
'For her red hair will bring bad luck!'
'Fuck off, ya baw bag,' I said and ran before I heard a
crack.

Ma Granny caught me swiftly and
crushed my heart with a hug.
'For auld lang syne,' she whispered, 'For auld lang
syne my dear.'

It's Curtains for Me!

Angela Haigh

It was 2010. Snow fell early and froze solid. A thaw shortly before Christmas allowed me to head off to see family and pick up my younger daughter who was spending Christmas with me.

The day we headed back to Scotland, there were warnings of heavy snow and sub-zero temperatures.

As soon as we crossed the Border, green fields and verges made way for wintry weather. My heart sank.

Once parked up outside my house, I found the ice prevented me from stepping away from my car.

The sky above was amazingly beautiful: but I didn't want to spend the night looking up, and I didn't want to break a leg.

I simply couldn't move. The house was a couple of yards away, but I wasn't ever going to reach it.

I may have wailed – hysterically - you understand.

Eventually, my daughter hatched a plan. Rummaging in her bag she brought out a jacket, laid it down on the ice and bade me walk over it.

'It's going to slip on the ice!' I shrieked - my panic rising.

'No; it *won't*. Mother! Do you *want* to stay out here all night? Look!' And she walked across it as if there was no ice at all. And again. And once more.

Holding onto to the car, I managed to make my way round to where she had laid the clothing and put a tentative foot on the fabric. It didn't slip!

It was now or never. I put a second foot down and remained upright. Wow!

Another garment was found and laid down. The first was picked up and placed in front, and so we made our way to the door, upright and safe.

My daughter went back to the car and used the frictionless surface to glide our bags and her other stuff across the ice towards me, now standing safe by the door, and so taught me a lesson I used for some years: whenever ice was outside my door, all I had to do was to lay down an old curtain to walk across; at least until I discovered ice grippers to attach to my boots.

Now ice and snow hold no fear!

It's Never Too Late!

Frank MacGregor

Andy Johnston shook out the pages of *The Annandale Herald* and turned to the sports page. 'Since when did you develop an interest in ballroom dancing?' he asked Jessie Allardyce.

'You need to get out of the house a bit more, and to tell the truth, you could do with losing a bit of weight,' she said.

When Andy's wife died his next door neighbours, Jessie and her husband Robert, decided to take him under their wing. This was Jessie's latest attempt at getting him, as she called it, involved. She had a point; he rarely ventured from the house other than to do essential shopping. It's not that he hadn't made attempts to get himself involved, he had. He just couldn't get himself interested enough in anything to stick with it. 'What made you think of dancing?' he queried.

'A poster in the library. I brought you a leaflet. Why don't you give it a go?'

The thing was, Andy wasn't sure he wanted to be bothered with dancing classes, but he didn't want to upset Jessie. It was far too late in life for him to be thinking about taking up dancing classes; he was past all that sort of thing, wasn't he. Still, he thought, maybe he would give it a go, if just to keep Jessie happy.

So there Andy stood, in Lockerbie town hall on a cold and wet Wednesday night, among a disparate group of would-be ballroom dancers. It had been a long time since Andy had felt the need to make an effort with his personal appearance; he was nervous. Would he have to make small talk, he wondered? He hated small talk. The thought of making a quick exit and going to the Kings Arms for a quiet pint was becoming increasingly attractive to him. The voice of one of the instructors put paid to his plan.

'My name is Jenny and this is my partner Tommy,' she said. 'Tonight we will start with the basic steps of the waltz. Would the gentlemen go to the top of the hall with Tommy, and the ladies stay with me.'

Tommy ran through the steps of the waltz with the men, and after half an hour, when he thought most of them had grasped the basics, he suggested they should return to the ladies.

'We're lucky,' Jenny said. 'We have an equal number of ladies and gentlemen. Your partner for tonight will be the lady or gentleman standing nearest to you.'

Standing next to Andy was an attractive, petite, silver haired lady. She looked at him, laughed, and said, 'You don't recognise me, do you Andy?'

For a moment his mind went blank. But there was something familiar about her. Then it clicked. It was Sheila Armstrong, they had been childhood sweethearts. It turned out that Sheila's husband had died about the same time he had lost Margaret. And like Andy, this was the first time Sheila had ventured out in ages.

Over the coming weeks Andy began to look forward, with ever growing anticipation, to his Wednesday night's classes. Sheila had become the very best of dancing partners, and a friend. Jessie commented on the difference in him. Now he had a spring in his step, she said. Maybe there was life in the old dog yet, Andy thought. What is it they say? "It's never too late."

Luck

Chris Openshaw

It wasn't a good start to my morning. I needed to get to the station at Lockerbie to help plant pansies there. One of my car tyres looked 'down' yet again. I'd been to the garage and used the machine to blow it up a number of times previously. Deciding it was a professional I needed now, I called in at the tyre place at the top of Bridge Street.

'Could you check my tyres, especially this one?' I said, kicking the culprit.

'Leave it with us and call back later, we'll see what we can do.'

Off I dashed to meet the others. I hate to be late, and at least it's all downhill. Planting done, then back up the brow to collect my car.

'It had a slow puncture, it's fixed, should be OK now.'

Back home, after a much needed coffee and still in gardening mode, I decided to mow the lawns while the weather was fine. It had been a while, the grass was higher than usual.

The front first, that's the easiest. Backwards and forwards, not doing badly although the grass was still damp and kept clogging the mower.

Front done, now the back. This proved harder; the grass grew longer here, the mower often stopping. Pulling the handle hard set it off again; this happened time after time until eventually the handle wouldn't work at all. 'Blast, now this needs looking at!'

First a puncture, then the lawnmower died, at least nothing else could go wrong … could it? They do say luck comes in threes whether good or bad; we'll have to wait and see.

Having to abandon the lawn my thought was to trim the hedges, the last cut of the year. Everything at the ready, extension lead, hedge trimmer, trug, brush and shovel. I started at the far side of the gate. The sun was high, getting hotter now. This side done, on to the next. Was it my imagination, was the strimmer getting heavier or was it the heat? Carrying on, wanting to get finished, I moved to the other side and started my first cut. Then, flash! Crackle! I looked at the end of the extension lead I'd just cut through. I couldn't believe it.

Looks like they're right, this certainly was my day for bad luck to come in threes.

Night

Kerrie McKinnel

I run until I'm sure he isn't following in the car, and then stop, hands on knees, panting. Darkness surrounds me. The rain is invisible against the black sky but I can feel the cold drops tingling on my skin.

I wait.

No car in the distance – I'd recognise the stutter of the engine a mile away. No ringing from my mobile. He isn't coming after me: final proof that he's an idiot (as if I need any more proof). Moving in together was a mistake. Daydreams and lingering kisses are no match for a derelict farm cottage with a broken toilet, and mice with a fondness for chocolate cake. No, it's just me, and the rain, and the darkness.

For a moment the only sound is me gasping for breath, and then I hear it – the roar of water. By the ice-blue light of my mobile, I leave the road and clamber down the bank, slippers sliding through mud like scissors through love letters. Brambles rip into the shins of my jeans. I jump the last four feet and land with a thud on the ground below.

The River Annan roars past my feet, swollen, battering at the loose bank. We used to walk along here when we were dating, pausing on the bridge holding hands to swap visions of our future – the farmhouse we'd renovate and make our own, the holidays we'd enjoy each summer to Greece and America and the Canaries, and the high-powered career which I'd put on hold to raise our make-believe children.

Thunder rumbles in the distance, barely audible over the water. I crouch down, kneel, and then find myself sitting, stones digging into my legs. With a sharp breath, I plunge my feet into the dark torrent. It seems like the only thing to do now. Maybe it'll help. I imagine the freezing waters washing away the last two hours, every word about money and stress which was thrown at me, and every sarcastic retort which flew from my lips in return. In the stifling heat of our kitchen it was as black and white as my mobile phone screen against the night. I was right, he was wrong. End of story. Now shut up and let me leave.

The light on my mobile fades. My eyes adjust to the night and gradually the shades emerge: blues, greys, greens, yellows, streaking and bubbling over my feet, sparkling on the riverbed, shimmering through the murk. My anger begins to slip, like soap from palms. Everything slows down in this deafening moment, this roaring, achingly cold moment, in this black night which isn't really that black after all.

I breathe out, feeling the rain pound my body, wishing I'd picked up a jacket but also beginning to wonder if our argument was like this night: not black and white at all but shades of right and wrong and somewhere in between, only obvious to those who take the time to listen.

Headlights poke above the horizon. As they near, I recognise the stutter of our car engine over the roar of the river.

Pulling the Wishbone

Kerrie McKinnel

'I won't see Steven and the grandkids until New Year,' said Betsy, flapping the creases out of a tea towel. Good drying day for December. She missed telling this to her husband, missed his colourful jumpers and scent of Old Spice, missed having a companion to walk to the park with when the sun shone, missed having a reason to cook a Sunday lunch from scratch. The days of keeping up with school uniforms, work shirts, and the inevitable orphaned socks were long gone.

'I've an idea,' cried Ada from the other side of the hedge which ran between the two gardens. 'Why don't we have Christmas lunch together?'

'Oh,' began Betsy, but Ada's eyes had lit up like advent candles.

'Why not? It's silly, the two of us sitting alone a few feet away from each other.'

'But, but ...' stammered Betsy. 'I've already ordered my turkey from the butchers.'

'Perfect,' said Ada, 'because I've got nothing except the brandy. Shall we say noon?'

Betsy's nerves grew as the day approached. In the five years since her husband had died, she'd made a point of phoning her son Steven and his family in New Zealand every Christmas morning to make sure he felt guilty for not spending the holiday with her, but secretly she'd become accustomed to her day. In the morning, she'd rustle up the only roast dinner that she bothered to cook these days. The wishbone, she'd always pulled with Steven ever since he was a child. In recent years she tended to set it on the side, meaning to keep it for his customary arrival on New Year's Eve but usually getting fed up of the sight of it and chucking it into the bin long before that. Christmas afternoon meant the Queen's speech and a nap, and in the evening the Christmas specials. Her grandkids made fun of her *Coronation Street* addiction but the regular characters had become a family to her.

Ada arrived at noon. Betsy served lunch promptly. The sooner it was eaten, the sooner she could regain peace.

'What a treat,' said Ada as she took the biggest slice of turkey and three sausages.

Those are Marks and Spencer's, thought Betsy, they're not cheap, but she didn't say anything. They'd shared a hedge for the best part of fifty years, having both moved to Lockerbie in their twenties to live with their respective husbands. Their sons were the same age and had been in the same year at school, but Ada's with the sporty crowd and Betsy's in the library. The boys passed all the usual events in coordination – birthdays, graduation, marriage, grandchildren. When the women were widowed within months of each other, that would have been the time to reach out, but Betsy was content with her solitary life.

Betsy ate in silence as Ada claimed the crispiest sausages, biggest potatoes, and chatted about Christmases past – the year the boys got water pistols and spent Christmas morning running about the slushy street in fits of laughter, and the winter when Lockerbie was snowed in, Betsy's boiler gave up and her family went to Ada's for the day.

'I'd forgotten about that,' said Betsy with a smile.

'And wasn't it magical,' continued Ada through a mouthful of stuffing, 'when the grandkids were here at the same time last year, throwing their footballs backwards and forwards over the hedge? They were at it all day.'

Betsy laughed out loud .

'Right, must be time for this,' said Ada, picking up the wishbone.

Betsy gasped in surprise and immediately put her hand over her mouth. 'But I usually keep that for ...' she began, and then stopped. For whom? For the husband long gone, or the son in New Zealand with his own family to spend the day with? She took a deep breath, let it go, and smiled. 'Okay,' she said. 'Let's pull it.'

Ada held up the v-shaped bone, turkey remnants clinging to the greying surface. The women wrapped their pinkies around it and pulled.

As Betsy waited for the snap, she wondered what she'd ask for if she was given one wish. That morning she'd wanted nothing other than her usual solitary Christmas Day, but now with a friend on the other side of the table, Betsy was beginning to think she could get used to this new routine. In fact, she wouldn't be averse to seeing more of Ada throughout the year. Maybe there could be Sunday lunches again, and walks to the park when the sun shone. Betsy closed her eyes, hoping that Ada might want this too.

Snap!

'Well done,' cried Ada, raising her brandy glass to the victor. 'What did you wish for?'

'I can't tell you that. Then it wouldn't come true,' said Betsy, standing to clear the table. 'Now let's get the pudding out, and then we can settle down for the Queen's speech. I don't suppose you like *Coronation Street,* do you?'

Tartan Journey

Steph Newham

Even though I was expecting her, I was startled when
Hilary spoke from the bedroom doorway. 'Coffee –
sorry I'm late,' she said, placing a mug on the window
ledge by my elbow.

I'd been staring down at the raised herb bed
bordering the patio. Now I lifted my forehead from
the cold glass. 'Mum's rosemary bush died last winter
and she never replaced it. I feel so lost – we didn't
know her at all, did we?'

'Of course we did.' Hilary threaded her way
across the floor through the piles of winter coats and
summer dresses and perched herself on the edge of
the bed. 'But it's difficult when we live so far away.'

I nodded, lifted a box of photographs from the
Lloyd Loom chair and placed it on the window ledge.
I sat, my hands around the warm mug, glanced at the
clutter on the bed and muttered, 'At least Dad doesn't
change. I couldn't believe it when he said, "I'm off to
our Dave's for a few weeks, you and Hilary feel free

to sort the House ...'"

Hilary laughed harshly. 'He meant, you two remove all trace of your mother before I get home. Christ he's got a bloody cheek. Cold fish. I can't understand why she worshipped him.'

'I don't think she did.'

'Don't be stupid, she idolised him and he treated her like dirt towards the end. What's the betting he had a bit on the side? It's him we don't know, never did. Everyone knew Mum, she was that kind of person…and what do you mean, we didn't know her at all? I certainly knew her, she called me at least twice a week with gossip about the Bowls Club and...'

'Oh yeah,' I almost snarled, 'and that was her life, was it? I don't think so, sis. If she ever told you she was happy with Dad, she lied. Take a look at these.' I got up, put my mug on the dressing table. 'I'll show you how happy she was.' I pulled a wooden cutlery box from beneath a pile of handbags on the bed. 'Shove along.'

It was a shabby box; utility, she'd called it. Cheap wood, flimsy, but she'd loved it. The cutlery had gone to a jumble sale years ago and been replaced by a Viner's stainless steel set, which she kept in a drawer in the kitchen.

'Do you remember the day we helped her remove the compartments and relined it with blue silk?' I asked Hilary. I lifted the lid.

'Yes, I must have been about eight, and you ten... She used to keep her poems in it. Are they still there?'

'Sure are, and more. As far as I can see, she doesn't seem to have written many after we left school; but wait till you see what I found this morning.' I rifled through a pile of programmes from shows she'd been to in Glasgow, and below them a few National Trust for Scotland leaflets. I finally found the poems she'd written for us as children.

'Fairies, and goblins, a spinning spider,' Hilary whooped. 'Ooooh I remember these.'

I shut the lid of the box with a thud. 'But you won't remember these.' I emptied the contents of a brown envelope onto the lid. Hilary reached over and picked up some of the contents: photographs of men in kilts, pipers, drum majors, programmes from Pipe

Gatherings across Scotland. 'There's a few letters.' I spoke slowly, carefully considering my next words, 'and what looks like a load of poems she was working on. The final letter's dated the week she went into hospital. She wouldn't have been able to reply to it.' I handed Hilary a photograph and some of the papers. Written on the back of the photograph, in our mum's loopy script, 'Lochmaben Royal Burgh Pipe Band, D. third from left top row.'

As she studied the photograph I said, 'The top sheet lists places she'd been to with that Pipe Band: Girvan, Carrick, Forres, Stranraer, Cullybackey (Ireland) ...'

'Blimey,' Hilary's mouth hung open. 'Christ, they got around...how come dad never twigged?'

I'd got no idea, but said, 'I think she must have said she was off with the Rural Women's Institute. He'd not be interested, never asked questions, all too easy for her. Take a peek at those and you'll see why we didn't know mum...'

Hilary put the photograph on the bed, looked at the first sheet of paper . 'Tartan Journey,' she said, reading aloud.

'I spy you, and the hot moment runs into a sounding swirl of stomping feet, that's how it is with you and me. A wiggle, back-slashed, tartan kiss. Drone my love on to the piper's sound, hearts found. Fond expression, kilten ranks in time together. I'll cheer my tartan piper, 'cauld wind' or nae.

'Eight yards, concertina'd, a short thread between us. A thought so thrilling, hidden in the pleats of my heart's desire. Hold me in a firm embrace. Like icicles you melt me with what's beneath the tilt of your kilt. Watch that wind, my marching man.'

'Flirt, send your sounds skirling, whirling about me. Later tease, a finger roaming across saliva-slicked lips. Yellow and green, blackly-watched pleats darken in a falling twilight. Belt cinched tight and calf flesh showing. Proper shoes with proper segs, deftly laced about your legs. Kilt swirling and twirling, brings on a swagger. Skinny ripples, guide you into my Loch. Wondrous piper of mysterious places. My one true love, our hearts' desire in time's embrace.'

In the silence that followed I said, 'His name's Donald.'

Hilary said, 'It would be. Not a trouser in sight, but I wonder why she hasn't finished them, seems as if she...'

Ignoring her, I picked up the letter. 'Listen to this. *"Dearest Jenny, the Lowland Gathering's to be in Paisley. I'll book a hotel as usual and as this year's something of a celebration, fifteen years – perhaps you'll have forgotten? – I'll book dinner for both nights. As a special treat I'm having a new kilt made, a bit longer, the old knees are scrawny these days. It'll be a fit setting for the wee dirk pin you sent me for Christmas, my love."'*

'Christ, a bloke wrote that to our mum.' Hilary slumped forward, flicked her hair back across her head. 'Christ, Dad won't believe it. Bet she never wrote a poem about him.'

'Dad won't ever know,' I said with all the force of an elder sister. 'But we have to reply, let this Donald know he's lost the love of his life.' I folded the letter, slid it into its envelope. Then I felt a smile pull at my lips, 'Dark horse our mum', but Hilary wasn't listening nor smiling. As I turned towards her she slumped into my arms and the box slid to the floor, its contents scattering. 'All that rubbish she told me about the Bowls Club,' she sobbed. 'If I'd really taken any interest she might have told me, told us about Donald, we might have encouraged her to…'

'No. She never finished the poems, she was on a journey, there was no end to her journey with him.'

Hilary hiccupped, 'I suppose so.' She leant down, picked up the photo and poems. 'What do we do with these?'

I stood up, crossed to the window and looked out. 'The sensible thing,' I said, 'is to burn them in dad's incinerator.'

The Floorboards Talk to Each Other in an Old House

Pat Mackay

'You know, he would have done it forty years ago if she'd let him, and we'd have been on the fire as soon as we went off the joists.'

'Yes, but she's always liked our wide boards. Now he's died, I think we're safe.'

'She's been looking closely at us lately, and she's talking of asking his apprentice to call in.'

'She's always talking about things, but she never gets round to them.'

'My side isn't so bad, but you shouldn't have let your corner get wet.'

'Now, how could I help that? She's let that conservatory roof leak for ages and I couldn't stop the water seeping under the wall.'

'Also, it was a mistake to let that visiting dog scrape a hole under the bed.'

'But it was an especially soft bit, and the dog had really long nails. I don't think she's noticed it anyway. There's another little hole on your side which is much more exposed. I've seen her looking at that when she sweeps.'

'We'll just have to hope she never gets round to asking that apprentice to call.'

The Flu Jab

Angela Haigh

Arthur turned into the car park; eight cars were already there.

'Pah! It's going to be way beyond my appointment time again,' he grumbled to himself, 'even though some of them must belong to the staff.'

He reversed the car into a space beside one identical in make and colour to his own.

'That might confuse somebody!' he thought gleefully.

He walked into the surgery. Two people were already sitting down, one on either side of the waiting room. There was no sign of the receptionist.

Should he ring the bell? There was a notice saying to do just that, but there was a deathly silence in the room.

'Ring the bell, make them jump; and me as well, probably; or stand here like a lemon? Some choice,' he thought glumly.

The two patients already sitting down had looked up in expectation as soon as he walked through the door.

'Like a bloomin' circus,' he thought. 'Oh! OK! I'll give them their flippin' fun! But shall I just give it a quick touch, or really let it zip?'

Gingerly, he put his finger down on the button:

BUZZZZZZZZZ! He jumped. The telephone at the desk rang at the same moment.

'Hope they enjoyed the spectacle,' he muttered to himself.

The receptionist appeared as if by magic, and answered the phone, leaving him still standing there, shuffling from one foot to another.

'The person at the other end must need a hearing test,' he thought irritably, as the receptionist repeated everything she was saying, time and again.

Finally, she put the phone down, only for it to start ringing again before he had the chance to open his mouth.

'It's been like this all morning,' the receptionist apologised, before dealing with the call.

'Now, how can I help?' she asked Arthur brightly, when all was finally quiet.

'I have an appointment at ten forty-five. Arthur Wilson: flu jab.'

The receptionist turned to the computer and logged him in.

'Nurse will see you shortly; we're running a little late, I'm afraid. Take a seat.'

As Arthur turned to look for a seat, the door opened, and in walked a harassed-looking mum with two active toddlers.

'Oh my! Bloody kids. That's all I need.' He kept his thoughts to himself, and sat down at a seat as far from anyone as possible.

While their mum booked in, the toddlers quickly found the box of toys. The older one, a boy of about four, picked out a car, and was zooming it up and down on the floor.

'She's probably here to get the kids some of that ... what's it called? Ritalin, that's it. Hyperactive nuisance!'

Arthur conveniently forgot about some of the activities he and his brother used to get up to at that age. They were far more "hyperactive" things than a bored toddler playing with a restricted selection of toys in a doctor's waiting room.

The next patient was called in, a man in his late twenties, wearing a t-shirt, jeans and trainers.

'Some skiver, no doubt; probably coming in for some methadone,' Arthur decided. He would have been shocked had he heard the discussion in the surgery about on-going testicular cancer treatment. The patient, far from "skiving", had just finished a twelve-hour night shift as a police officer, much of it dealing with a fatality on the road not far from Annan.

Arthur glanced irritably at his watch; already gone eleven.

'Mr Wilson,' came the call from the nurse's room.

Arthur slowly got to his feet: he had always had a needle phobia and would have happily avoided this appointment if his daughter hadn't threatened to bring him here herself.

'Good morning, Arthur. All ready for your flu jab? This won't hurt a bit!'

'Morning Nurse. You know and I know that's not true! What is it some of your colleagues say? Ah yes, "*a sharp scratch*". Don't know why I have to have it anyway - I never get the flu!'

'Probably because you have your flu jab!' replied the nurse calmly. 'Now, roll up your sleeve, whichever arm you prefer.'

Arthur realised he couldn't put it off any longer, and glumly rolled up his left sleeve.

'I'm not keen on needles,' he muttered, before his eyes rolled into his head and he fainted.

When he came round, he found the nurse checking his blood pressure.

'Well, Arthur. That was quite a performance! I was just about to ask doctor if we needed to send you to A & E. Now, shall we get this injection done? Your obs all seem fine. Good job not everyone reacts like that!'

Before Arthur could protest, the nurse had done the deed and was sticking a small round plaster on his arm.

A subdued Arthur found he couldn't think of any suitable retort, so meekly left the room. When he walked to his car, he was confused as to why the key seemed to be faulty, as it wouldn't open his car. Looking up, wondering if he had the breakdown number in his pocket, he realised the little prank he had done as he arrived. He scurried to the car adjacent to this, relieved to find the key worked perfectly.

The Two Sheep

Chris Openshaw

This poem was inspired by the installation of sheep statues in Lockerbie town centre, and written to mark St. Valentine's Day. An earlier version of this poem was published in The Annandale Herald *newspaper in February 2014.*

We're always together, just you and me,
standing on the square at Lockerbie.
We only met a few months ago,
since then we've stayed here
through rain and snow.
Although we don't say much,
in fact nothing at all,
we will both stay together
watching Lockerbie Town Hall.

The Weather

Chris Openshaw

It's six o'clock. I turn on the TV, the weather forecast is on next. I'd better watch it to see what the week ahead has in store.

The weather map for South Scotland shows that tomorrow and the rest of the week will be the same. We are to have unsettled weather, chilly with showers, some sunshine, cloudy with winds approaching from the west. A bit of just about everything.

Well, it is Scotland.

Now I can plan my week. It looks like it's staying inside for me, getting jobs done indoors and forgetting about the garden.

On waking up the following morning what do I find? The sun shining, albeit not very strongly. I look across towards the hills: blue skies with scudding clouds coming this way.

So bang go my plans, at least for today. I'll work with the weather, put on my gardening gloves and get outside.

Then I'll see what tomorrow brings.

Well, it is Scotland.

GHOSTS AND THE
SUPERNATURAL

A Ghost Story

Pat Mackay

I expect the family had watched a few horror films before they moved here. Theirs was the only two-storied house in the village. It stood on its own facing down the valley, attractively framed by climbers and large trees.

Any film producer would have chosen their house to be the haunted one. The only sticking point might have been the age of the family. A horror film usually features a young family, but this one was old enough to have produced five children, albeit rather close together. However, our producer would have been encouraged by the fact that the mother spent many evenings alone. The father worked away during the week and often attended sporting activities at the weekend.

The mother came to visit us and tell us about the first strange event. She had gone upstairs to check that the children were sleeping peacefully and had found the two youngest awake and excited. They told her that a man had come through the wall and spoken to them. They described his appearance in detail, particularly his drab clothing. The mother recognised it from their description as the uniform of a soldier in the First World War. She settled them back down and then tried to sleep herself – pricking up her ears for the sounds of any more soldiers coming through walls.

The next night, my husband and I were invited down to spend the evening in the haunted house. We drank homemade elderberry wine and listened to the story again. I felt the hairs rising on the back of my neck. We heard a noise in the hall and left the sitting room to investigate. There was a chill in the hall (it was a cold stone house with no central heating), and a malfunction in the electricity supply was causing the meter to go backwards. However, the children slept soundly that night.

After that I had to go down to London to arrange some work. I believe my husband visited the haunted house again but saw nothing unusual.

A few weeks later, we were lucky enough to hear another side of the story from our neighbours, the minister and his housekeeper. They had received a letter from a woman whose brother had died in the First World War. This woman and her brother had lived in the "haunted" house; she had a strong feeling that her brother now wanted her to bring his poems and diary back to the village.

We told the mother to speak to the minister, and the sister was encouraged to come and visit the house with her brother's poems and diary. She had tea with the children and shared photos of her brother. The diary was written very small and kept in a cigarette tin. The sister left the diary to the local school, knowing that this would have been her brother's wish.

After her visit, the minister blessed the house and the family were able to live there in peace.

Had this been a film, who knows how many regiments of soldiers would have passed through that wall before the end of the story?

A Ghost Story

An Overpaid Fare

Richard Sharp

It was a damp morning as he headed down to the river. Walking down he stopped for a moment and put down his fishing tackle.

A faint wisp of mist hung in a line over the autumn river. He reflected to himself that the Annan was somehow more direct and straightforward than rivers he used to fish when he was younger and living in the Midlands. Those rivers had broad and gentle curves, and stretches where trees dipped in and out of view and indeed in and out of the river. Slower to rise and fall. Calmer.

But somehow he liked the Annan, harder to fish but more direct. Somehow more honest. Quicker to rise and fall. Angrier.

But enough of this reflection, he said to himself. Since his recent retirement he had sometimes found himself drifting off into thoughts and reflections, where before he would rush from one situation to another. Now he seemed to be organizing his thoughts. Putting them in order.

Later, when he had set up his tackle and was about to start fishing, he did something he had always done since he had started fishing as a child.

He threw a coin into the river.

He didn't know why.

Superstition? But it had become a habit now, every time he went fishing. He half thought that it would bring him bad luck if he didn't do it anymore.

It must be a small fortune by now, he chuckled to himself.

When evening came he started packing up. It was going to be a long walk back up the hill. The thought of it tired him. There was a sharp pain in his arm, he rubbed it. He ought to make an appointment to see his doctor.

Perhaps his wife was right, he thought ruefully. When he told her he was having a problem with some twinges in his chest she was quite insistent. Indigestion, he said.

Still that was for another day. Today had been the best day's fishing he could remember. Throughout the day, he had caught a steady succession of trout of increasing size. Today had been special.

He smiled to himself. *I could die happy if this was the last day's fishing I had.*

Picking up his fishing tackle, he felt a sudden cold chill from behind him and he shivered.

He turned round and saw a figure walking towards him. He or she was well wrapped up against the cold with a hood hiding their face. 'Evening,' he said, surprised to see another person.

There was no acknowledgement of his greeting. Approaching closer, the figure reached towards him holding a coin in an outstretched hand. A dusty voce quietly said, 'Here, this is yours. You have paid more than enough.'

The following day they found him floating face up in the river. His fishing tackle was on the bank.

Heart attack, they said. They were sure of that. But what they couldn't explain was why he had a smile on his face and why his fist was tightly clenched around a coin.

An Overpaid Fare

The Pen

Frank MacGregor

It was cold and wet, and a thug of a north wind was cavorting through the high street like an escapee bull from an abattoir. And to cap it all, I still had three hours to kill before I caught my train. With rain inveigling itself into almost every orifice of my body, I wondered what the hell I was going to do for the next three hours. Then I saw the poster. There was to be an auction – antiques and bric-a-brac, the poster said – but more importantly, considering the weather, the auction was being held that very day.

The sale room was hot, steamy, and crowded – probably with poor sods like me desperate to get out of the rain. As I ploughed my way through a jungle of stacked furniture and artefacts my eyes settled on the most beautiful Victorian writing box I had ever seen. Brass escutcheon plates and reinforced corners, two screw-top inkwells, original blue leather with a gold-tooled writing surface, and a hazel brown coromandel graining that drifted across the box like smoke curling from the embers of a dying fire. It was love at first sight. Anyone who has attended an auction knows the auction fever that can assail the most sanguine of us. I made all the usual resolutions: I would not bid, I would watch and see how much it fetched, my interest would be purely academic. That's what I told myself. Then the fever took hold. In short, I bought the box.

Writing boxes are known for hidden secrets. As soon as I got home I began to fiddle about in all its nooks and crannies to see if I could unlock its secrets. When I pressed the bottom of the right hand inkwell recess, a spring cover revealed two secret drawers. In the left hand inkwell recess there was a small indentation. I applied a little pressure. Bingo, there was a third secret drawer, and this one wasn't empty. Nestling inside was something wrapped in tissue paper. I carefully unwrapped it. Inside the wrapping paper lay a fountain pen. Not any old fountain pen, it was a Waterman's Ideal, a collector's item. I couldn't wait to try it. I put the nib into the ink bottle, gingerly lifted the lever and started to draw ink. Perfect, not a leak. I dried the nib, took a piece of paper, and wrote my name; the pen floated across the page.

When I acquired the pen I was living in the small town of Lockerbie, situated in the Scottish Borders. I worked for the local council and most of my leisure time was taken up with my poor attempts at writing a novel. One night, not long after acquiring the pen, I decided I would have another go at my book. From the moment I picked the pen up and wrote the first sentence I knew something strange was happening. Gone was the compulsive need to re-read and re-write. There was no hesitancy, no doubt. The plot unfolded before my eyes. Characters came alive; they spoke to me, they told me what they should say and how they should say it.

Over the following weeks I existed in a frenzy of inspiration. I couldn't sleep. I neglected everything. I lost my job. Chapters flew from the pen. The book was completed in three months, all eight hundred pages of it. It was proof-read, typed, and submitted to a leading literary agent. Don't ask me why, but I knew before I sent it that it would be accepted.

My name is Jonathan McFarland, you may have heard of me. My book, *Convocation*, was nominated for the Booker prize.

I used to dream, in my genteel poverty, of owning a bolt hole, a retreat, somewhere I would have the luxury of writing without distraction. Now I had the financial wherewithal, I determined I would indulge myself. I bought an idyllic old cottage, situated just north of Inverness. After three months on an endless promotional treadmill of TV, radio, and book signings I was exhausted. All I wanted to do was find a quiet place, pull the silence around me and vegetate. I headed north.

As I drove up the long twisting track that led to the cottage I had the uneasy feeling that all was not as it should be. I got out of the car. Everything looked fine. I walked to the rear of the cottage; the back door had been forced. It hadn't occurred to me, when I bought the cottage, that this level of quiet and solitude comes at a price. My cottage, my sanctuary, had been well and truly screwed. The writing box was gone and so too the pen.

I was contracted to write a follow up. No need to be fazed by that prospect, I reasoned. A follow-up book would be no problem. After all, hadn't I a mountain of research work to draw on? I began to rationalise the loss of the pen. Maybe it wasn't just the pen. So I started to write again. It went well, at first, but then got more and more difficult.

I sent the opening chapters to my editor. Her response was not unexpected: 'The first five chapters are fine, Jonathan, great stuff, but the other five don't seem to gel; the narrative is less confident and the characterisation is not as sure footed. I will call you at the weekend and we can discuss it in more depth.'

As I write, the book remains unfinished. I am attempting to finish it, but it's not the same. When I sit staring at a blank page, desperate for inspiration, I find myself thinking about the pen. Is it sleeping in its secret drawer, I wonder, or has it already found another aspiring author?

The Pen

HISTORICAL
CONNECTIONS

Harvesters

Chris Openshaw

I could hear the harvesters laughing as they worked. The sounds coming from over the hedge, out of the field next to the path I'm walking along.

I stop and kneel down to spy between the hawthorns. Something's funny, they're all so jovial. Just what am I missing, not being able to hear properly? I can't even guess. How I wish I could join in with their merriment but of course I can't, I'm only a lad and they are men fully grown.

Can I get nearer? Maybe I can find a gap to crawl through. Found one! I lie flat and begin to wriggle my way in. Stop! My shirt's caught, careful now, unhook myself, if I tear it I will be in bother when I get home. No harm done, I'm loose now, must take my time, squirm a bit further through to the other side. Keep still. Has anyone seen me? Don't think so. Stay quiet, move slowly and listen out.

The harvesters have moved further away now, I'll creep along the hedge and try to get nearer. What if I'm spotted, how will they react? Shouldn't be here, will I be in trouble? I'd love to be amongst them, laughing, the fun, the summer sunshine; can't wait to grow up and be one of them.

Should I ask if I can help? Would they show me what to do, just to learn a little of what happens on this side of the hedge?

My mind wanders off, thinking about my future, hoping it will be here. I can't imagine anything better. I feel a hand coming down on my shoulder. I jump, startled. What now? I stand frozen.

A voice behind me asks, 'And what might you be doing here lad?'

'I heard you laughing and making merry. I was hoping to join in and be part of it all.'

'What about the work?'

'I won't mind about that, I'll work hard, I promise.'

The hand moved around my shoulders but now in a more friendly manner. 'Come along, young man, and let's see what you can do.'

I'm here with all the men now, just a boy being allowed to help with the harvest. In the field, in the sunshine, among the laughter.

Moss Wall

Steph Newham

Many of our Clan dispersed from the lowlands to
Australia, crammed into the holds of sailing ships,
weaving far-flung places into our family cloth. For
these last few days in Hobart I wrap myself in
Armstrong plaid before I start my own long journey.

Stories have a life of their own – my story is
ending. Spindles twirl – threads of family unfurl. Here
on my balcony overlooking the harbour, I shuffle my
travel papers aside and move on to the pile of family
documents. I run my finger down a list. On my dad's
side, Effie Armstrong, died 1743. Donald Armstrong,
her cousin, died 1759, both stitched into new
colonies. Here are the Kerrs listed in a neat hand in
my mother's journal. Ewan Kerr, married Emily 1846;
four children: Douglas, Mary, Margaret, Ewan. Only
the boys survived childhood to produce new roots in
a strange land.

An interweaving of clans, the Armstrongs and
Kerrs live on in my mind. Shadowy names from my

mother's journal and my on-line research. I have not betrayed her faith in me. The tree she started is finished. I have no child to pass it on to; I am a last link in a long chain. I am the last of our Armstrongs and I have decided to take the family in my heart home to Eskdale before I weaken.

****

She kept her eyes tight closed, used her fingertips to explore the old stones. Her hand trembled in the cold; she jagged a nail on a piece of granite. She was tired but happy; I'm glad I came, she whispered, pressing her lips lightly against a cornerstone, feeling the spring of wiry moss against her cheek. As a young girl she'd heard tales of her Scottish ancestors. Poor relations, they had fished and farmed, even raided – scraped a living from this wild bog land. She was the last of them. She had travelled from Australia, back to this northern land. Close in the shadows of the crumbling walls she reached back in time, felt herself cradled in the arms of her clan.

The ground beneath her was cold, moisture glazed her jacket. Shivering she pushed her hands into her pockets. She slid the hardness of the sharp flint into her palm, then sat, rocking gently to the ripple of the river over its pebble bed.

Despite the cold her brain still fired; images of goddesses, mythical beasts, fighting stags and tartan-clad swordsmen danced across the insides of her eyelids. Over the last few months she had discovered her mind to be both a dark vortex and a place of refuge.

The disclosure by her consultant had not been a surprise. She was easy with death, it held no fear. Life was finite. History and mythology were her passions; both had taught her the uselessness of craving immortality. She would miss the joy of instilling that love into her pupils. Her research field, The Goddess Cult, had always been strong in her as a resource for life.

The Goddess Artemis had helped. It had not been easy to find her. She had sought her in wild, inaccessible places; listened for her in the windy rustling of the eucalyptus trees of the wilderness, searched among the pebbles and rocks on white sandy beaches, roamed isolated acres of arid outback. Finally, she heard the Goddess's voice inside her own head, spurring her on: sell up, move out, make this journey. Find your true home.

Now crouched among the crumbled remains of the bothy, she felt for a sense of belonging. She sniffed in the pungency of damp moss and cold earth that supported the remaining walls; ran her finger tips over the mossy stones where dead voices gather, was reassured.

She was the last – too few sons, barren wives. Spinsters like herself had abounded. A spinster with terminal cancer that a double mastectomy had been unable to forestall. She was sad that the many-breasted Artemis had not chosen to stem the cancerous fecundity of her disease.

Despite her illness, her last few months in Hobart had been good – she'd felt alive. She had bathed in the beauty of each sun-baked day. Her mind leapt about like the flash of pink parrots in the park.

Ideas tumbled and jumbled themselves until that day she decided she'd reject further intrusion by the scalpel. She would go home; home to Scotland to die.

It had been easy enough to arrange. She was to be buried among the Armstrongs here in Langholm. She might have wanted a little more time: to explore Eskdale, to feel the press of emotions that clung to the fabric of this ruin she had found. She would share her death with the stones that had sheltered and protected her ancestors, let her blood seep into the ground to feed the vegetation that clung on in the confines of the old walls.

Always unpredictable, she chose to die here, to die free. Disease would not tame her. She chose to die in darkness, to feel this night's autumn chill curtailed into a bitter winter. She felt the coldness of the flint in her hand. Listened to her ancestor's whispers; long forgotten tales of the passion of a wedding night, pain of childbirth, loss of a husband and child, the fear of leaving this land.

It was done. She shrank against the mossy stones, inhaled the rustiness of damp peat. She heard whispered voices and a distant skirl of pipes. The sounds flowed through her, mingled with her blood seeping thickly red into the ground beneath her.

Moss Wall

Scotsman's Stump

Chris Openshaw

All around were fields, different shades of green and I could smell ... onions, just a hint, a trace catching on the breeze.

'Can you smell onions?' I asked my walking companion and workmate Joan.

'It's the wild garlic you're smelling, it's probably growing over there in that copse.'

I'd not heard of wild garlic; she'd been country walking before but this was the first time for me. I was sixteen, spreading my wings, doing something different, feeling very grown up.

We'd worked out the journey in our lunch hour yesterday. Now it was Saturday, the weather fine, so armed with backpacks of drinks, sandwiches and the map, we caught the bus to Rivington Village on the outskirts of Bolton. Then on to Rivington Moor and our destination – Scotsman's Stump.

'I know it stands at the top of the hill,' said Joan looking at the map. "Not too far I hope, but we've all those fields to pass first though."

We walked slowly, taking in our surroundings, noticing sheep and lambs, no other walkers about; just us, the peace, the quiet and the vague smell of garlic.

The moors were much bleaker now than when we'd first set out. The path we were following went as far as Blackburn, miles away according to the map.

'That must be it up ahead,' said Joan, picking up speed towards a metal post at the side of the road. We both stood there and read the inscription on the pillar.

GEORGE HENDERSON

TRAVELLER

NATIVE OF ANNAN, DUMFRIESSHIRE

WHO WAS BARBAROUSLY MURDERED

ON RIVINGTON MOOR

AT NOONDAY NOV 9TH

1838

IN THE 20TH YEAR OF HIS AGE

'How awful, I'd like to know more about that poor man,' I said.

'Let's look into it when we get back,' Joan suggested.

We'd reached our goal, had our sandwiches and drinks, trekked back to the bus for home, then later to the library. No Google then.

Finding further information about the murder of George Henderson, it seems it was a big thing at the time as the horror spread throughout the area. He was working as a salesman for a Blackburn draper, and was walking the same path we'd followed when he was shot and robbed. They never did convict anyone for his murder; they did have a suspect, but no real proof. A tree was planted by the locals on the spot he died, but was later replaced in 1912 with the iron pillar that stands there today.

Thinking back now to George Henderson and the moors of Bolton, his fate has taken on more importance for me as the years have passed. Back then, just a girl of sixteen growing up in Lancashire, the names and places meant nothing to me. I had no idea that one day I'd set down my own roots in Dumfriesshire. These days, I'm reminded of him each time I look at his native hills, or smell the wild garlic that grows along the lanes.

Scotsman's Stump

MODERN FAIRY TALES

The Dragon of Annandale

Paula Nicolson

Thank you to Eskrigg Nature Reserve, Lockerbie, for the inspiration behind this story.

Once upon a time, deep in the heart of the kingdom of Annandale, there was a dragon. He was a beautiful and kind-hearted dragon who lived in peace among the villagers of a small market town in the east of the kingdom. The dragon's favourite place to visit was a small pond in a wood just outside the town, and in the depths of their cold and icy winters, the surface of the pond would freeze. The local villagers took to playing and fishing on the frozen pond. However, early in the morning before anyone was awake, the dragon would sit by the pond and throw stones across its frozen surface to see which one would go the furthest. Although a simple game, it kept the dragon and the young animals from the wood amused whilst their parents cleaned out the nests and foraged for breakfast.

On one such day, the stones the dragon found were not sliding far; being irregular in shape and bumpy, reduced their speed and range. The young animals, who he also chatted to, soon lost interest and began to wander off to find more exciting things to do. Fed up, the dragon struck upon the idea of travelling a little further to find some smoother stones.

The dragon flew off across lowlands and highlands, the land and the sea; losing track of time and feeling tired, he decided to rest on a small island off the coast. On this island were birds, flowers and animals that were completely different from any he had ever seen before. They told him that he had landed on "Ailsa Craig", an island that was originally part of a volcano and was blessed with many magical properties. It was said that fairies would often visit the island to gather magical spells, and that is why it became known as the "Fairy Rock" or "Ailsa Craig". After accepting food and drink from the friendly dwellers, he rested for the night in a small cave by a beach.

The next morning, the dragon took a short walk along the beach to take in the fresh, salty air. As he strolled along the water's edge, he came across a few beautifully smooth, rounded stones; they would be perfect for playing his skimming game at the pond, he thought. He collected a pawful of stones in a seaweed pouch, but just as he was about to fly off, a fairy appeared beside him. She asked the dragon where he was taking the stones to. When he explained, she frowned, but agreed they would indeed make powerful skimming stones; however, she was worried that others would return to take more and soon there would be no stones left. The kind-hearted dragon promised that he, and others to come, would only take as many stones as they needed at the time, so that the island had enough time to recover and make more. The dragon and fairy embraced and as the dragon bid farewell, the fairy blessed the stones with her magic dust so that they would slide even more. After arriving home in the dark, the dragon settled down to sleep, excited by the thought he could tell his woodland friends about the island he had discovered, and the new stones.

The next morning, he sat by the pond and threw the stones across its frozen surface; they worked perfectly! To add a little more interest to the game, the clever red squirrels and the bossy robins made two circles on the pond's surface, with the innermost circle named a "target". They all competed to see who could slide their stone as close to the centre of the target as possible. The animals and birds found this so much fun that they didn't notice a little girl who was watching them from behind a tree, drawn by all the noise they were making. As she became more and more captivated by their game, she came out from behind the tree and stepped towards the edge of the pond. It wasn't until she said 'Can I play?' that they realised they had company!

Startled, the animals and birds dropped the stones and slipped and slid away across the pond; soon, no one was left but the dragon and the girl. 'Can I play?' she repeated and noticing that she had been impolite, blushed and added, 'please'.

The dragon agreed and rolled two stones into her upturned palms. The little girl and the dragon played all morning together under the watchful eye of the woodland creatures that had taken cover under the tree canopies.

In time, the little girl and the dragon became very good friends, and once a week they would play with the stones together. As the little girl grew up, local villagers would pop by and join in. The dragon would often fly back to Ailsa Craig to collect a few more stones. Remembering his promise, he never took too many. Once he even had afternoon tea with the fairy, who blessed his stones again with her fairy dust.

When the dragon died, the villagers decided to continue to play the game in his honour and called it "Curling". The townsfolk continued to use the granite rock from Ailsa Craig for their curling stones and each one was blessed by the local fairy. They became very good at it and shared the game with other townsfolk from around Scotland; they even set up competitions in which they won many prizes.

In time, the locals moved their game to a different place and gave the pond back to nature, but they continued to win prizes all around the world, even to this day. Legend says, that if you sit by the pond on early frosty winter mornings and listen carefully, you can hear the chinking of stones and feel the warmth of the dragon's breath as he plays with the stones he found on Ailsa Craig.

The Dragon of Annandale

The Grass Troll who entered the Talent Contest

Paula Nicolson

Dedicated to Natasha Gilfillan who gave me the inspiration to write this story.

Down by the River Annan there once lived a Troll, a Grass Troll in fact, on account of his bushy green hair; his name was Eric. But unlike most other Trolls found in fairy tales, this Troll was a thoughtful "Guardian" of his particular patch of the river.

His daily tasks included helping young puddocks hop in and out of the river by means of ladders he had made from plaited willow. The toads were a bit trickier to help, as they often left smears of their foul tasting slime on the ladder, much to the annoyance of the Bank Voles (who shouldn't have been using the ladders anyway). Eric's other tasks included helping the red squirrels find their nuts when they lost them (which was quite often). He had even won an award for keeping the river banks clean and tidy from the "Trolls for Tidiness" Society.

One sunny day, Eric was sunbathing on top of a bird hide. He was feeling very proud of his swimming trunks made from a sweet wrapper, when he was interrupted by a neighbouring Grass Troll. 'Ye ken there's a talent contest up at Grass Troll HQ? Whoever wins, gets to marry the princess. It's going to be called "Troll Land's Got Talent". Fancy entering?' Eric paused for thought, he was pretty nifty on the banjo. 'Aye, where do I sign up?'

Half an hour later, Eric had put in his application, but he wasn't really interested in marrying the princess. He wanted the runner-up prize of a tent with solar lighting, for he liked to read at night. As the competition was to take place the next day, he decided he must put in some practice. A Bank Vole, a puddock and a heron volunteered to sit on the "panel" and after an afternoon of banjo playing, they agreed that he was a thoroughly good musician.

The next day, Eric finished helping the last puddock out of the river and skipped up to Troll HQ. The air smelt of roasted chestnuts and fruit punch, and was filled with the chatter of the local wildlife who were debating about who was going to win. Eric headed backstage and once there, was surprised to see the competition he faced: juggling elves, singing pixies, and a few trumpet-playing fairies. As Eric was not on until later, he decided he would take a quick snooze and be fresh and ready for his act. However, he was soon awoken by a beautiful young lassie Grass Troll shaking his shoulders and shouting, 'They have moved some of the acts around and you are now on in ten minutes!'

'Thank you,' he replied. 'But where is my banjo?' They both looked around but it could not be found; Eric thought it must have been one of the fairies, as they were always "borrowing" things for their own homes, especially teeth.

The lassie Grass Troll, who introduced herself as Esme, felt very sorry for Eric as he seemed such a nice Troll (and he had lovely blue eyes too). 'What are you going to do? Do you have any other talents?' she asked. Eric talked through a number of ideas and together they hit upon an alternative: he would tap dance because he had always been good at that when he was a youngster. He sent a message via the wood pigeon to ask if his squirrel friends could bring his tap shoes up to the show.

In the meantime, Grass Troll HQ agreed that Eric could appear later on as there had been a last minute entry for a banjo-playing fairy. Esme even did an act herself: she managed to juggle four squirrels without dropping any of them (only their nuts). Finally, Eric's friends arrived with the tap shoes. Esme wished Eric good luck and kissed him on his cheek; he was so stunned that someone so lovely could give him a kiss that he nearly didn't appear on stage – were it not for some swallows (who dragged him on by his coat).

The audience at Grass Troll HQ had never seen a tap dancing Troll before. His act went down so well it received the most votes from the audience and the panel, and he won the contest!

To his surprise, Esme admitted that she was in fact the princess! Eric and Esme got married and lived happily ever after in a tent, with solar powered lighting, by the banks of the River Annan.

The Ring of Annandale

Richard Sharp

(Apologies to Wagner and Tolkien.)

It was a clear spring morning on my walk round Castle Loch.

I had stepped out onto one of the fishing platforms to take in the view. But after a while my reverie was interrupted by a muttering sound.

Looking about me, I saw a very small bearded figure with a red pointed hat, fishing from the end of the platform.

'What are you staring at?' he snapped.

My first thought was, I'm staring at what appears to be a gnome fishing. But something in his grumpy demeanour made me hesitate.

'Haven't you seen a gnome fishing before?' he snapped again.

Only as a fairly ironic kitsch ornament in a garden centre, I thought. But again this didn't seem a particularly apt comment.

'Caught much?' I asked, whilst immediately thinking, what a stupid thing to say.

He looked up at me with a derisive glare that could have turned water into stone at three hundred paces.

'Caught much! I'm not fishing,' he snorted.

He proceeded to pull in his line, a thick string attached to a large stick on which there was a large hook. Then he recast the line, slowly dragging the hook across the bottom of the loch.

He repeated this action several times.

Seeing my bemused look, he said, 'I'm trying to find it. I WAS out fishing yesterday and I lost it. The ring of Annandale, you must have heard of it. The ancient ring of power forged in gold from the deeps of the River Annan.

'Stupid human!' he said, noticing my blank look.

By this time, his disdain was making me feel as small as him, so I attempted to come back with a knowledgeable comment.

'I've heard of the One Ring that rules them all and the ring from the Rhine that gives power over the Earth.'

'Bah! Too much hype. Mere trinkets,' he laughed out loud.

Noticing my bemused look, he explained, 'The Ring of Annandale is more powerful. Well, more fun anyway! The wearer can make anyone or everyone forget whatever he wants them to forget.'

Noticing my still puzzled expression, he went on.

'Look, it's a lot of work ruling the world. All that power. Underlings here, there and everywhere. All that organising. Things don't run themselves. You never get any time off.

'No, with this ring you can do anything you want and no one's the wiser. Crop circles, Stonehenge, Easter Island statues. I've done them all. No one remembers who, how or why. See?'

I had to admit I was beginning to see that world domination may not be all that it's cracked up to be. Especially when compared with a gnome's sense of humour, when I noticed something shimmering in the shallow water by my feet. Reaching down I pulled out a golden ring that shone brilliantly.

'The Annandale Ring,' he cried excitedly. Snatching it from my hand he put it onto his finger, pointed towards me and smiled.

It was a clear spring morning on my walk round Castle Loch. I wish I could remember what happened next.

NATURE

A Sight to Behold

Angela Haigh

For ten months, Ali and Mark had been in a long-distance relationship, having first met each other through work. They were now engaged and had just spent a number of hours in Dumfries completing their Christmas shopping.

As they drove back to Mark's home in Gretna, Mark said he had a surprise for Ali. He took a different route home before parking up near the Police Station.

'Why are we stopping here?' asked Ali.

'Don't worry,' he smiled, 'it's absolutely nothing associated with the Police.'

It was not long before sunset on a bitterly cold afternoon, and the sun was shining.

'We'll wait in the car a short time,' he told her, 'and see what happens,' he continued mysteriously.

Ali saw that other people had gathered. They were looking into a field – no, they were looking skyward. Some had cameras in their hands, others tripods set up.

'Are we going to see some shooting stars or something?' she eventually asked, her curiosity piqued.

'Nope – aha ... I think we can get out of the car now.'

Ali followed Mark, curious to see what everyone was looking at, but all she could see was a small flock of birds in the air.

'Mark: why have we stopped to watch a few birds?'

He kissed her gently, and told her to keep watching. Over the next few minutes, the flock was joined by more and more, creating an enormous flock that seemed to fill the sky.

'They're starlings, Ali – just in case you're not sure?'

'Okay – so why have we come to see some birds when I can see them any time I like back home?' she asked, shivering and beginning to feel a little exasperated.

Mark hugged her and smiled mischievously.

Eventually the sky around them was filled with hundreds, perhaps thousands of birds, dipping and weaving, sometimes forming patterns that resembled whales or fish or dense mathematical shapes, a living, pulsating black cloud.

'There's a peregrine!' someone in the crowd shouted. Ali followed the pointing finger and watched as a larger bird, intent on its supper, seemed unable to pick off just one from this the mass around it.

'How come it can't just stretch out a claw and grab one?' Ali asked, surprised.

'The starlings are constantly moving, and the peregrine wants to fix its eye on just one – but it gets confused. It will probably get one eventually.'

As well as the amazing aerobatics being performed overhead, their ears were continually assaulted by the clattering of wing beats and the constant cacophony as they called to each other.

'They come to Gretna to do this nearly every year. A lot of them are birds from mainland Europe – they aren't all local birds at all. In fact, starlings are considered to be in danger worldwide; their numbers are dropping massively.'

'You wouldn't think so, looking up there,' said Ali, impressed.

Suddenly somebody swore good-naturedly.

'I think that man's been got at!' grinned Mark.

'Got at? What on earth are you talking about?' queried Ali.

'There are a lot of birds up there – some say maybe half a million; I'm not quite sure how they count them though! Can you hear those noises on the road?'

Ali listened a few moments, then looked at the road in the dimming light.

'You mean I could be heading home covered in starling poo?' she exclaimed. Mark grinned again.

Far above them, the birds continued to swoop and dive as the setting sun made its way inexorably towards the waters of the Solway. They flew lower and lower, concentrating now on woodland, and over the next few minutes, they came down in groups, dropping like rain, landing in the trees, and chattering noisily. Suddenly the sky was empty, bar one peregrine falcon that was flying away from the roosting birds, a starling gripped in its talons.

'It got one then?' she declared sadly.

'They have to eat too.'

'I guess so.'

'One bird out of nearly half a million – it won't harm this particular population at all, and will keep that peregrine alive for another day.'

A Sight to Behold

A Swear Word

Chris Openshaw

In the Dryfe Valley there's a cottage on the edge of a village. Each morning the lady living there goes out to feed the birds. You can see her every day after she's breakfasted, washed up and tidied away, coming out of her home carrying a dish filled with bread already broken up into bird size pieces. In her other hand a plastic cup full to the brim with bird seed.

She walks along the path towards the gate. Waiting for her on the other side is a male pheasant; he knows why she's there. Opening the gate, she crosses the road to some spare land where they are fed. A robin sits on a branch nearby and a blackbird's waiting in the wings, they both know what's ahead.

Making clucking noises she sprinkles the bread around first, then some seed. From the far hedge, out of the long grass come running more male pheasants followed by the females, about nine in all. She goes back to her garden and uses the rest of the seed to refill the bird feeder hanging from the bush. Later a pair of pheasants will come to catch the seeds dropped there.

Her daily routine means that the pheasants and other birds get closer to her. They're not afraid now, and are used to the clucking noises she makes.

One morning two males were first to arrive; one picked up a piece of bread then the other jumped at him to warn him off. The first male took his bread to the side but time and again the second one would try to domineer.

The lady was incensed, her voice rose, and instead of the usual clucking she shouted at him, 'Pack it in you greedy bugger, there's enough for everybody,' then looked around to see if anyone had heard.

He knew who she meant, his neck went up, his head twisting round while the other carried on eating in peace.

Mornings since then are back to normal. Just the usual quiet feeding with her gentle cluck, clucking, at least until next time.

Autumn

Chris Openshaw

From my window I look out and see
What was my beautiful sycamore tree.

In the summer, deep coloured leaves.
Now it's Autumn, what's left of these?

Pale russet brown catching in the wind,
Taking flight over everything,

Landing on hedgerows, grass and the path,
Lying there going brittle, until at last

I collect them up to put in a bag,
Until next year when I will be glad

To have some leaf mould to use on the land,
And my sycamore back to looking grand.

Brief Encounter

Angela Haigh

Selina fed the cats, then set about making her own breakfast. She still missed the breakfast walks she'd shared for so long with her beloved dog Max, who had died some weeks earlier.

'One day, Max, I will get another puppy, or maybe a rescue dog. I hardly ever walk our walks nowadays. Mind you, the rain we've had all summer hasn't helped; everywhere is so muddy, or full of puddles.' It was a poor excuse really, and she knew it, but walking those same tracks without Max hurt too much.

However, it wasn't raining today. In fact, it was quite a pleasant autumnal morning: blue sky was visible among the white clouds, though rain was forecast before lunch.

'So, what can I do today?' she pondered. She had been retired now for almost a year, and when she had Max, there was still some routine in her life.

Selina considered her options. She could catch the bus down to the next village, just over a mile away, go to the woods with her camera and see what she could see, be it wildlife or just the autumnal changes, then walk back. Yet somehow, walking back was far more of a challenge than walking there. However, living in rural Dumfriesshire, there wasn't a regular bus service, so she could only catch the bus in one direction.

'Got it!' she smiled. 'I'll walk down when I'm ready, head to the woods and see what birds are around; I may even see a red squirrel! Without the dog bounding about, always wanting to chase a squeaky toy, perhaps there will be some sign of them. Then I can catch the bus back.'

Having made a satisfactory plan, she was able to sit down and eat her breakfast, while watching the birds on the feeders.

'There's definitely more and more greenfinches returning after the moulting period,' she mused. 'I do miss seeing the swallows though; I wouldn't mind spending winter in some nice sunny climate like they do.'

Selina had always had a passion for animals of all kinds, and was as happy to watch the sheep or cattle in the fields beyond her garden as the birds. She recalled the previous spring, watching the lambs with their endless chasing games, while the half-grown cattle would follow each other like teenagers in a shopping centre, before all lining up and looking over the fence, seemingly discussing the washing on the line.

Selina glanced at the clock and, deciding she really should be setting off soon in order to catch the bus back, hurriedly rinsed the breakfast dishes, before considering what to do about a coat.

In the end, she simply put an umbrella in her rucksack, deciding that the walk would soon warm her up.

Selina loved autumn. The sun shining on the autumnal leaves gave them a rich colour she could barely describe.

'Orange and yellow are totally inadequate,' she thought, 'while russet doesn't describe all the variations.' The rowan trees, hawthorns and wild roses had rich red berries, while the brambles still had lots of large black ones, ideal for a crumble.

'I might come and pick some later,' she thought. 'I forget about these now I'm not walking Max anymore.'

A shadow fell across her face, but not for long, as she came to a field with a donkey and her half-grown foal.

'You two are beautiful!' she said, thankful for the chance to catch her breath. 'Mind you, how something so beautiful can make such a racket, I'm not sure. I heard you braying when I was in bed!' As if on cue, the mother started up again. 'Sorry; I can't stop any longer. I want to give myself plenty of time in the woods!'

She walked steadily uphill, occasionally stopping to see what was in the fields, or admiring flowers in the verge. Before long she reached the top. Looking ahead, she could see two young mums with buggies walking towards her, heading back to the village after taking their older offspring to school; they exchanged a quick hello as they passed.

The downhill stretch was much easier, though the thunder of three timber wagons roaring past in quick succession reminded her to report the pot holes that had re-emerged in the road: the patching-up job only done in the spring hadn't even lasted as long as the swallows!

Selina spent a few minutes on the bridge over the River Esk, rewarded, as she gazed upstream, with the sight of a heron standing motionless in the water. She heard two oystercatchers scream above her head as they flew downstream before landing in a shallow section of the water.

She got her camera out and took a few pictures, before deciding it was time to head towards the woods.

Away from the traffic, the first bird sounds she heard were confined to the happy chatter of sparrows and the territorial calls of two robins, but before long, she had left the village behind and was soon walking among the trees.

Tall, spindly silver birch, their leaves just turning yellow, nestled alongside the richer orange and gold of sycamore. Occasionally, a leaf would flutter down, joining the small pile along the verge. Cut logs awaited collection, but Selina could see no notices restricting walkers, despite heavy machinery parked up close by.

She stayed still a while, letting her ears tune in to the sounds around her: the traffic on the nearby A7; an occasional sheep bleating. Then finally, she heard the sounds she had come for: once again, two robins singing their melancholic territorial song, one immediately answered by the other. Eventually, Selina was able to locate the nearer of the two, and took a picture. The sudden shriek of a jay interrupted her, but was impossible to locate. The crowing pheasant was far easier to see, and then the *pink-pink* of a great tit in the trees made her look upwards. No sign of it, but way above her, two buzzards glided lazily in the thermals.

Selina watched them for a while, before remembering that she wanted some pictures of the trees in their autumn colours, so she wandered around, locating different types of tree, snapping a few that were not quite yet in their full autumn glory.

Suddenly, quite close to where she was standing, she heard a rustling in the undergrowth. Expecting to see a pheasant emerging, she held the camera ready: a blackbird's alarm call seemed to confirm her suspicions, though as yet, she saw nothing.

Again, a slight rustle; Selina stood still and silent, and then peered closely into the undergrowth. Her happy mood instantly changed to one of dismay.

'Oh no! Surely not?'

A third time the rustling was heard, and she wildly clicked the camera; shot after shot after shot. But she didn't really need any digital evidence. She knew what she had seen, and so she slowly turned away, deciding to walk back for the bus. Her morning's outing now seemed to be totally ruined.

What should she do? She toyed with the only two options available. Keeping quiet was the easy one. Nobody else was around; nobody knew what she had seen. Or should she.....?

'NO!' The thought screamed in her head.

She couldn't. She wouldn't. How could she?

When she got home, Selina, still upset by the brief encounter in the woods, recalled the pot hole that needed repairing, so, logging onto her computer, she looked up the number for the council.

'Dumfries and Galloway Council. Stuart speaking. How can I help you?'

'Hello. My name is Selina Collins. I'm not sure who I need to speak to, but I'd like to report a pot hole that needs repairing.' She took a deep breath, before continuing: 'And I would like to report a grey squirrel I have just seen in a cull zone.'

Sometime later, a mug of tea in her hand, Selina struggled with her conscience: had she done the right thing? Grey squirrels passed on a virus - lethal to reds, though not to the greys. By reporting the grey, in a cull zone, she was passing on a death sentence. However, the red could die if she said nothing, and the virus caused a slow and painful death to the native squirrel. She acknowledged to herself that she'd had to do it; by doing so she may have helped to save a local population of reds.

Finally, she could smile again.

Dreaming on the Banks of the Annan

Steph Newham

Staring across the Solway, you slide into daydreams, your mind wallows in coffee mud and you imagine a drowning man reaching out to you. You know he will strangle you with his panic if you attempt to try and save him. But you clutch at him, don't let him go. You hang on, your fingers clasping his arm through the fabric of his jacket. You feel cold water tug and eddy at his body, sucking him into salty sea-green swirls; a pregnant swell surges through the newly-dredged channels as you strain to prevent yourself being pull into the fast flow.

You remember once hearing someone in the pub say, 'The Annan will still take a few days' downpour for this kind of flood to get the debris out of the river.' A whooping swan breaks the spell; you start – your eyes fasten on a bobbing log escaping from the Annan. 'Liar,' you think. For one moment you imagine the river emptying a body into the Solway. A body you did not save – and your dream dies too.

Home

Chris Openshaw

From the door
along the path
past the bush
the bird feeder
smell sweet peas
through the gate
turn right
follow the Dryfe
to the corner
around the back
past the sheds
reach the gate
I am back home

The Annan's Flow of Life

Kath J. Rennie

A version of this poem was published in 2001 under the title The Annan's Flow, *in the anthology* Poetry on the Lake, The Silver Wyvern Award. *The original anthology had been gifted to my mother. In 2013, after her passing, the book was returned to myself. Having spent many hours on the river banks with my mother, I decided to revisit the poem, changing it slightly to give extra depth and meaning.*

There's a magical river
That is...
Heaven's ornamental bliss,
Where colourful hues camouflage nesting chicks,
Natures circle of life bewitched,
Instinctively carrying on
The state of being at one.

One in life
God's seeing
Surviving the course unto its end

All Being.

Swan Mother sits on love below.

Warming is her touch, nurturing growth,

Patiently caring,

Patiently sharing

The blueprint within,

The blueprint from Him.

One in life

God's seeing

Surviving the course unto its end

All Being.

Light cascades from the waters-fall

Reflecting the power, the call,

The pull toward another place

Beyond far-off-hills, blessed with grace,

Beyond fruit-bearing trees

Swaying with the songs of bees.

One in life

God's seeing

Surviving the course unto its end
All Being.

Man-made Bridges
Erected on strengthened ridges
Housing birds of flight
And creatures of the night...
Architecture genus in glory
Forever to keep own stories.

One in life
God's seeing
Surviving the course unto its end
All Being.

Vastness greets the river's end
A sea of many blends...
An ocean of life decreed
To never concede...
A wonder of the world
Totally unfurled...

One in life

God's seeing

Surviving the course unto its end

All Being.

The Annan's Flow of Life

The Shepherd and his Flock

Kath J. Rennie

Fields aflush with crystallized dew
presenting to my eye
a palette of glorious hue...
Splashes of buttercups,
open petals to greet the sun,
whilst daisies in their multitudes
bow and curtsey
each and everyone...
For wintertime has passed,
its foreboding darkness,
the harshness of snow
blanketing the hills of Tundergarth,
those high
and low.

A blackbird appears,
hunger has her fight
through trenches of sodden ground
sifting amongst debris with all her might,

chasing off those around...
The sparrows;
the jays;
rooks; en-massed
she stakes her claim;
an early worm is grasped.
And another, then a insect or two
until startled into flight
by the farmer who,
on his quad-bike, stood high
seeking one from the flock.
A sheep who was nigh
delivered to him a shock:
he'd expected twins,
she'd gave him three
beside the old, old chestnut tree...

With hands of care
Lammac jackets on each are placed
giving the lambs the best start in life
and the Ewe accepts with grace...
Once satisfied all is well,
home then the farmer does go

for an hour or so, to take his bread

and maybe, hopefully,

an hour in bed.

For some early birds have had no sleep,

especially in springtime

as the Shepherd of Sheep.

ON WRITING

The Problem with Characters

Steph Newham

They have no heart, these characters of mine,
squeezing my ego into nothingness,
until I let them speak. They are
superior beings imposing their views,
forcing their words onto the page;
dictating actions I have not planned,
contesting the routes I would lead them.
Stubborn, deceitful, fickle fellows,
they shock me with their language,
then upbraid me for my mediocrity,
insist I have no other life, go nowhere,
do nothing independently, attend
them constantly. Explore the gamut
of their emotions, record their lives.
They allow me to think all goes well –
then insolently confound me.
They change my style, confuse me,
let me struggle in their rejected shrouds
cloaked in the madness of the story they write.

The Drive Home

Richard Sharp

Driving back from the Writers group at Lockerbie. Yet again thinking, what on earth could I write about for the next group meeting?

I could write about coming up to Scotland about twenty five years ago, and why.

Or I could make up a story of ghosts and ghouls.

Or a poem about light and dark and the shades of good and bad.

But none of them would do. They sounded so trite and, well, just a little bit hard to write.

Still, I thought, something will come.

So, driving back along the road out of Lockerbie to Lochmaben, a journey I'd driven many times before. On my right the Garden of Remembrance for the Pan Am flight.

On my left the walk in the woods to the Nature Reserve; remembering walks with my children.

Then following the bend at the top of the hill, looking west across the valley.

A panoramic view with broad lush fields and scattered trees. Sometimes as I drove home from work the sunset would be red and glowing, pointing me homewards.

Down and across the five-arch bridge over the Annan. Always noting the river level. If I'd been away for a few days, I could easily tell, by the height of the water, what the weather had been doing in my absence.

Now the long stretch of flat road. Almost always a buzzard by the roadside. If the fields were flooded there would often be swans grazing and at least one heron, sometimes more.

And then to my left, Castle Loch. History and kings and queens and ghosts. But for me it was the place where I caught my monster bream after a lifetime of trying. Perhaps next time it would be the monster pike, if the otters I'd seen didn't get her first.

Then into Lochmaben, with a street so broad, almost continental. There at the end, the statue of Robert the Bruce. His birthplace? Who knows?

Then on to Mill Loch. Iron age crannogs. A deep cold loch. The last home of the vendace, a fish now extinct.

Then home and looking out of the window seeing a couple of roe deer grazing over the back of the garden.

I stopped to think for a moment.

Perhaps, after all, it was not so difficult to find something to write about.

BIOGRAPHIES

Angela Haigh is a retired science teacher who worked in both Yorkshire and Cumbria.

From being an avid reader, her writing interest developed and began more seriously from 2005.

She had a daily blog running for a number of years with the News and Star, and joined an international online writing group together with a local one at Eskdalemuir.

She has achieved some success with short stories in online writing competitions.

Angela has so far completed two books of a trilogy, which developed simply from a personal writing challenge.

She joined the Lockerbie group early in 2014.

Bryan Armstrong is an editor at the DnG Media publishing group, which includes the Annandale Herald, Moffat News, Annandale Observer, Dumfries Courier and DnG24 news website.

Chester-born, from a Scottish family, Bryan, who lives near Annan, has never been far from words, ink and paper. From delivering newspapers as a teenager, completing a printing course in Dundee and serving his apprenticeship as a compositor, his journalistic career with DnG Media includes spells as a photographer, reporter and assistant editor before taking up his current post in 1994.

Chris Openshaw, after finishing work three years ago, joined Lockerbie Writers group. Her inspiration comes from her background in Lancashire and latterly from the countryside in which she lives.

Frank MacGregor is a retired business man and lives with his wife Marjorie in Lockerbie. He has always had a lively interest in history and is currently in the throes of writing a novel centred around the seventeenth century Scottish civil wars.

Godfrey Newham is a retired publishing editor, keen reader, music lover and hill-walker. He has lived in Annan since 2013. He believes that good editing is the key to presenting good writing, and hopes that this anthology will encourage readers to share his belief.

Kath J. Rennie was born in 1955, on a British Army Camp in the Country of Wales. A mother of three sons and a step-son. Grandmother of four granddaughters and two step-granddaughters. Kathleen lived in the City of Manchester for twenty-eight years, before moving to the town of Lockerbie, aged thirty.

Besides motherhood; she has worked in the Nursing/Caring profession, and became interested in complimentary therapies, qualifying in 2004 in Reflexology.

Art & Design had always been her hobby and after attending George Street School of Art, in the town of Dumfries, this became her path after retiring, as too, writing again.

Kerrie McKinnel is a writer and student on the University of Glasgow's MLitt Creative Writing. In 2015, her writing was included in two anthologies, and her poem, *The Enchanted Forest*, featured in a sound installation during the Dumfries Christmas

Lights Switch-on. Her fiction is inspired by beaches and forests, dog walking and chocolate, and the occasional fleeting memory of what life used to be like before toddler tantrums and board books.

Kerrie lives in rural south-west Scotland with her husband and son. She recently completed the first draft of her debut novel.

Kerrie writes a blog about her experiences of writing and her upcoming publications, which can be found at:

www.kerriemckinnel.wordpress.com

Lewanna Stewart is an artist/illustrator currently living in Boreland near Lockerbie, having recently moved north from Cornwall where she did an M.A. in Illustration/Authorial practice. Often found working on her own self-initiated projects from comics to screen printing, she welcomes work for commission for the pleasure of collaboration and the opportunity to explore and develop the work of others through the medium of drawing.

More examples of her work can be found at:

Pat MacKay has lived in Dumfries and Galloway (Annandale and Eskdale) for the last forty years. She has been writing regularly for about three years. She has two daughters and one grandchild.

Paula Nicolson is a scientist by day, but a writer by night. She loves creating poetry and making up stories for her daughter, and finds her inspiration from the Dumfries and Galloway countryside, contemporary art and her eccentric family history. Paula hopes her stories and poetry will bring a smile to your face and fire the imagination of children.

Paula also writes a blog on life in Dumfries and Galloway which can be found at:

www.facebook.com/deckywriting

Richard Sharp has no ambitions whatsoever to be a writer but likes playing around with words and seeing what happens. An avid reader whose favourites range from Charles Dickens to Thomas Pynchon. He is an occasional angler and is desperately trying to learn how to play the piano after a lifetime wishing he could.

Steph Newham took up writing when she retired from the NHS. She did a Cert in Creative Writing followed by an MA at Lancaster University. She is currently working on a collection of Short Stories as well as a historical novel. She is chairperson of Lockerbie Writers and a member of Powfoot Writers. She has had articles published in newspapers and short stories in an anthology and on-line e-zines. She enjoys running workshops and encouraging others to develop their writing skills.

Lockerbie Writers, 8th March 2016.

This photograph was taken in the Kings Arms Hotel, Lockerbie, as the group nearer completion of their anthology.

Back Row, Left to Right: Paula Nicolson, Kath J. Rennie, and Frank MacGregor. Front Row, Left to Right: Angela Haigh, Steph Newham, Chris Openshaw, and Kerrie McKinnel.

Photograph: Copyright © Kerrie McKinnel.

Lockerbie Writers' meeting, Autumn 2015.

This photograph was taken in the Kings Arms Hotel, Lockerbie, during one of the group's regular meeting.

Left to Right: Kerrie McKinnel, Chris Openshaw, Paula Nicolson, Frank MacGregor, Richard Sharp, and Angela Haigh.

Photograph: Copyright © Steph Newham.

Lockerbie Writers' meeting, Autumn 2015.

Another photograph taken in the Kings Arms Hotel, Lockerbie, during one of the group's regular meeting.

Left to Right: Richard Sharp, Angela Haigh, and Steph Newham.

Photograph: Copyright © Steph Newham.

Lockerbie Writers' Christmas Lunch, 24th November 2015.

This photograph was taken in the Kings Arms Hotel, Lockerbie. Left to Right: Frank MacGregor, Chris Openshaw, Kerrie McKinnel, Richard Sharp, Paula Nicolson, Angela Haigh, and Pat Mackay.

Photograph: Copyright © Chris Openshaw.

LOCKERBIE WRITERS GROUP

Do you enjoy writing?

Lockerbie Writers are a relaxed and friendly
group that meet every other Tuesday in the
Kings Arms Hotel between 10am—12pm

Come along for a cuppa and try out an exercise to
stretch your imagination and skills!
Beginners are very welcome and you don't have to live
in Lockerbie to join.
Contact: Steph on 01461 758247

Lockerbie Writers' Anthology:

Stories and Poems from

Annandale and Eskdale

and other retail outlets.